100 THINGS
TO KNOW ABOUT
ARCHITECTURE

happy yak

Brimming with creative inspiration, how-to projects, and useful information to enrich your everyday life, quarto.com is a favorite destination for those pursuing their interests and passions.

Inspiring | Educating | Creating | Entertaining

Author: Louise O'Brien
Illustrators: Dàlia Adillon, Leanne Daphne
Designer: Sarah Chapman-Suire
Commissioning Editor: Carly Madden
Editor: Nancy Dickmann
Creative Director: Malena Stojić
Publisher: Rhiannon Findlay

First published in 2022 by Happy Yak,
an imprint of The Quarto Group.
The Old Brewery, 6 Blundell Street,
London N7 9BH, United Kingdom.
T (0)20 7700 6700 F (0)20 7700 8066
www.quarto.com

A catalogue record for this book is available from the British Library.

ISBN 978 0 71127 266 8

Manufactured in Singapore COS072022

9 8 7 6 5 4 3 2 1

100 THINGS TO KNOW ABOUT ARCHITECTURE

LOUISE O'BRIEN

DÀLIA ADILLON
LEANNE DAPHNE

happy yak

CONTENTS

Refer to the glossary on pages 110-111 for an explanation of any tricky words or phrases.

INTRODUCTION

Hello, budding architects! You are about to experience the wonders of architecture, which is the art of designing and constructing buildings. From schools and skyscrapers to palaces and castles, prepare to travel through history and around the world to discover the most exciting architecture ever.

100 Things to Know About Architecture shows how architects use their imaginations and technical skills to create all sorts of buildings for all kinds of purposes, including for living, working and worship. Discover how simple and complex shapes are used in architectural designs, learn about ancient and modern masterpieces, then marvel at eco-friendly buildings of the future. Inside this book, travel to China to see a Tulou, to Italy to see a Dome and Brazil to see a Favela. Discover a Riad in Morocco and a Ryokan in Japan.

So, what are you waiting for? The creative, global world of architecture is just a page turn away...

Yanomami Village (Venezuela)

Bibury (England)

Sulawesi (Indonesia)

VILLAGE

· ·

For thousands of years, humans have lived in small communities called villages, where villagers relied on easy access to local water and building materials. This means that villages across the world look different, depending on the climate and local materials. Often, villages in hot climates have timber houses with big roofs, such as the rows of bamboo buildings with saddle-like roofs found in Sulawesi, Indonesia. In parts of Venezuela, round timber buildings called *shabonos* house over four hundred people each under one curved roof. In Bibury, England, buildings made of local golden stone keep people warm in the cold winters.

Burj Khalifa (Dubai)

Shanghai Tower (Shanghai)

Empire State Building (New York)

One World Trade Center (New York)

Petronas Twin Towers (Kuala Lumpur)

Willis Tower (Chicago)

International Finance Centre (China)

Shanghai World Financial Centre (Shanghai)

SKYSCRAPER

Skyscrapers are symbols of modern business. Towering skyscrapers have shaped the skylines of cities such as Hong Kong, New York and Dubai. The first skyscraper was built in 1885 in Chicago. The architect used a strong, lightweight steel frame instead of stone, making a 10-storey building possible. Since then, we have reached for the clouds! Shanghai Tower in China is 632 m tall, and the Burj Khalifa in Dubai is 828 m high – that's 163 storeys! The skyscrapers of the future will form forests of cutting-edge towers. And they'll have sustainable designs to remove pollution and create a better future.

LEGO®

....

Lego comes from Danish words meaning 'play well'. Lego is the world's most used construction toy – there are about 400 billion bricks in use worldwide! Lego encourages creativity and patience, at the same time as developing engineering skills. With Lego, you can quickly build whatever you imagine. The colourful bricks can be used over and over, each time making something completely new. Designed by Danish architect Bjarke Ingels, the home of Lego – Lego House in Billund, Denmark – opened in 2017. Lego fans can visit this house, which was designed to showcase the fun creations you can build using just Lego!

Habitat 67

PIXELATION

· ·

Digital photographs, found on your phones and computers, are made up of tiny squares
called pixels. Architects are inspired by pixels, which become cubes when they are made
three-dimensional. In 1967 Moshe Safdie designed the first pixel building – called Habitat 67 –
in Montreal, Canada. After making a model from Lego, the finished version had more
than 350 concrete boxes stacked to form apartments. The unusual layout created outside
balconies, giving each apartment access to light and fresh air. Today architects around the world
are using pixels in their buildings. Who knows what our cities will look like in the future?

Casa Batlló

ART NOUVEAU

Around the start of the 20th century, designers took inspiration from nature. They developed a new style, called Art Nouveau, and soon it was everywhere: in art, posters, jewellery, architecture and more. Art Nouveau made use of flowery, swirling shapes. It celebrated nature with designs that looked like butterfly wings or growing plants. Entrances to the metro stations in Paris look like giant vines and strange insects. In Barcelona, Antoni Gaudí used his imagination to create a vibrant masterpiece unlike anything ever seen. It's called Casa Batlló and has an ornate design, all the way to its colourful, tiled roof.

Chrysler Building

ART DECO

The 1920s and 1930s were an exciting time in design. This was the age of Art Deco, where you could see geometric shapes, zigzags, streamlined shapes, fans and stepped pyramids inspired by ancient buildings in the Middle East. The 319-metre Chrysler Building in New York City, designed by American architect William Van Alen, is an example of the magnificence of Art Deco. The building's special feature is its shiny spire made of layered crescent shapes. The building is one of the world's most famous skyscrapers – a symbol of New York at a time when it was beginning to really boom.

Living root bridge (India)

Juscelino Kubitschek Bridge (Brazil)

Golden Gate Bridge (USA)

Sydney Harbour Bridge (Australia)

Millau Viaduct (France)

BRIDGE

Bridges are structures that connect a path or road across land or over water. The first bridges were as simple as a log fallen across a stream, similar to bridges made from tree roots in India. Today bridges can be more complex and they can come in different forms. The Sydney Harbour Bridge, which is a through arch bridge, and the Golden Gate Bridge, which is a suspension bridge, are world famous for their designs. The world's tallest bridge is the Millau Viaduct, which is taller than the Eiffel Tower. Its height and complex cables make it a beautiful sight.

Sendai Mediatheque

STRUCTURE

Without a strong skeleton to hold it up, your body would flop around like a jellyfish. A building also needs a 'skeleton' to hold it up, but this structure is made of sturdy columns instead of bones. While structures have an important function, there is no reason that they can't also be beautiful. In 2001 the Japanese architect Toyo Ito designed a library called the Sendai Mediatheque. It has a structure that looks like tree trunks. Ito wanted the library users to feel they were inside a modern forest, with the steel columns growing up like trees through the library.

Heydar Aliyev Centre

DAME ZAHA HADID

. . . .

Dame Zaha Hadid was born in Baghdad, Iran and studied architecture in London. Thanks to her groundbreaking designs, by the time of her death in 2016 she was one of the most talked-about architects in the world. Hadid built eye-catching projects around the world and was the first woman to win the Pritzker Prize and the Royal Gold Medal. She created her own architectural style, often called parametricism, which makes use of computer-aided design tools. Hadid's buildings use curved and angled lines to create designs where edges disappear, and walls and floors become one. Her buildings are always uniquely Zaha.

Shanshui City design

TOPOGRAPHY

Topography is a fancy way of referring to the layout of a landscape. The innovative Chinese architect Ma Yansong, who trained with Zaha Hadid, uses parametricism to design buildings that blend in with nature. The curved shapes of the buildings produced by his company, MAD Architects, are futuristic and awe-inspiring. The buildings often appear to grow out of the landscape! Some look like mountains or rock forms, while others resemble waterfalls or sand dunes. Balconies and overhangs are designed to look like rice terraces and mountains. These buildings look as if they are alive or moving, and connected with nature.

BIODIVERSITY

Earth is home to a huge range of living things – that's biodiversity. Did you know that biodiversity and architecture are linked? Building cities and structures can damage the environment, but architects are working to reduce their impact on the planet. They use the latest science and technology to improve the building process and make it more sustainable. Experts on plants, trees, wildlife and rivers work with architects to find ways to protect what we have, and to fix what's been damaged. By connecting architecture and nature, we can find a way to coexist with wildlife and create thriving, healthy communities.

TREEHOUSE

· ·

Humans have been building and living in treehouses for about 40,000 years.
The jungles of Papua New Guinea are home to the Korowai people. High up in
the banyan trees, they build platforms where people can sit and sleep. But why
live in a tree? A tree provides a ready-made structure that provides stability, and
living high in the canopy gives people safety and a good view of the ground below.
Treehouses appeal to adults and children alike. They are an instant adventure – you
can create a getaway in your own back garden and have fun high in the trees.

Sydney Opera House

SYDNEY OPERA HOUSE

. . . .

After its design won an international competition, the Sydney Opera House was constructed between 1959 and 1973. The Danish architect Jørn Utzon came up with the sail-shaped design – perfect for the building's location in Sydney's harbour – and the British engineer Ove Arup helped turn Utzon's vision into a reality. Utzon and Arup studied different geometric curves before settling on a series of arced spheres that formed spectacular shells. The building's shape was something that the world had never seen before. As well as being an architectural marvel, the Sydney Opera House has become a proud symbol of Sydney and Australia.

National Museum of Qatar

SCULPTURAL

. . . .

Sculptural architecture is when architects design a building as a living sculpture that people can enjoy, not just as a practical object. All buildings are three-dimensional, but not all buildings are sculptural. Artists, such as painters, think about space and light and how the viewer will see their creation in its surroundings. Architects do this as well! Opened in 2019, the National Museum of Qatar by French architect Jean Nouvel is a one-of-a-kind living sculpture. Inspired by a type of crystal, giant discs interlock at different angles to create a really inviting sculpture that people can walk through and experience.

Eden Project

ECOSYSTEM

An ecosystem is a community of plants and animals as well as the environment where they live. The different parts are all interconnected. The Eden Project in Cornwall, England, is designed to showcase different ecosystems. The spectacular glass domes, called biomes, create the climates needed for plants to grow and flourish. The design looks like futuristic bubbles! There are two domes, forming a rainforest biome and a Mediterranean biome. The Eden Project is designed to protect, inform and inspire. The architecture shows how science, nature and engineering can merge to create beauty, reminding us that together we can protect Earth.

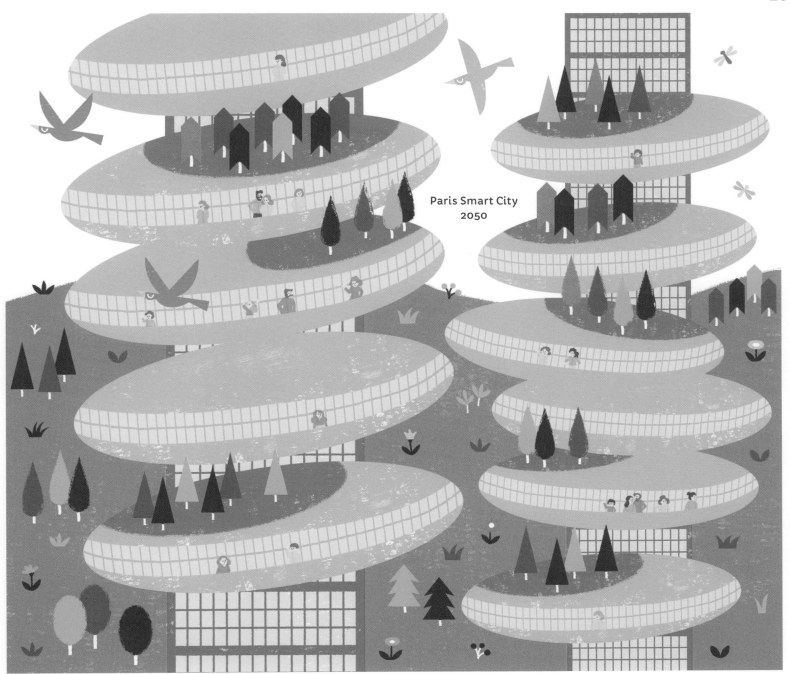

Paris Smart City
2050

HIGH-DENSITY

We often think of a home as sitting on its own small block of land. But with a growing population, architects are now looking for ways of encouraging high-density living. This simply means packing a lot of people into a relatively small space, but ensuring that homes are still comfortable and appealing. If all of your shops and schools are within walking distance, and you can use public transport, that's a more sustainable way of building a city – no more new buildings spreading over the countryside. High-density living is a way of ensuring that green areas are maintained and protected.

3D printed house

3D PRINTING

Architects make models to show what their designs will look like. The architects often build them from cardboard, but some use a 3D printer instead. These printers use plastic, metal or other materials to 'print' a solid object. Kae Woei Lim is an architect who loves 3D printers so much that he now trains other architects to use them. 3D printers can print more than just models. Since 2017, 3D printed homes have become a reality. It's a very exciting new way of building. In just 24 hours, 3D printers can print foundations and walls. These printers are inspiring innovation.

MICROHOME

Not everyone wants to live in a big mansion! Microhomes, also known as tiny homes, are a new way for people to live big but think small. They are more convenient and require less cleaning than standard houses. They are also better for the planet.

A microhome must be multifunctional, allowing the occupants to sleep, work and relax in one small space. These tiny homes use space-saving tricks, such as pull-down beds, walls that can move and furniture that folds up. In Japan, architects are creating truly innovative microhome designs. In the future, perhaps we will all live in one!

Guggenheim Museum

THE SOLOMON R GUGGENHEIM MUSEUM

GUGGENHEIM MUSEUM

The Guggenheim Museum in New York was designed in the 1940s by Frank Lloyd Wright – possibly the most influential American architect ever. On the outside, the museum resembles an upside-down pyramid made of curving shapes. This bold choice really stands out against the tall grids and rectangles of New York's skyscrapers. The building is made of reinforced concrete with no supporting columns in sight, so everything seems to float. Inside the building, gallery visitors walk along a long spiral ramp as they take in the museum's collection of modern art, while light pours into the atrium through a huge skylight.

Bilbao Guggenheim Museum

FRANK GEHRY

In Bilbao, Spain, there is another Guggenheim art museum with a design that's just as groundbreaking. It was the brainchild of Frank Gehry, one of the world's most popular architects. Some say that Gehry's creations truly represented the 20th century. Gehry's unique style of architecture makes use of grand sweeping curves and bold compositions. His buildings are made of bricks and metal, but they look as if they could move. Gehry's designs are inspired by music, art, technology and more. The fantastical shapes make each site a beautiful place. In turn, the buildings inspire us with the power of architecture.

WELLNESS

There's an old saying that 'an apple a day keeps the doctor away' – and maybe a well-designed building can do the same! Architects can improve people's lives by creating spaces that are calming, positive and healing. Spaces that make use of colour, daylight and views of the outdoors can activate the five senses, making people feel energised and refreshed. Creating calm spaces where people can unwind and escape has the potential to improve the way they feel and think. Hospitals now consider their patients' overall experience, recognising that the building itself can actually help the patients feeling healthier and happier.

15 min.

10 min.

5 min.

M

WALKABILITY

Healthy cities can create healthy people. If pavements, streets and buildings are designed beautifully and laid out sensibly, city dwellers will walk more and enjoy their city. People who walk in their neighbourhoods, to school or work, feel more connected with their local community. City planners are now seeing that prioritising walking over making space for public transport can have significant health benefits. Streets can be safe when they are full of activity. Creating pleasant footpaths, instead of more roads for cars, will reduce air pollution. This will improve people's fitness and give people more opportunities to enjoy the outdoors.

INCLUSIVE

· ·

When we describe design as 'inclusive', it means that it's people-friendly, considering all kinds of people and their needs. Inclusive design celebrates difference and is meant for all, regardless of ability, age, culture, gender or race. It is carefully designed so that people who need assistance can access buildings and facilities. Architecture must serve all users, including children and the elderly, people with poor eyesight, autistic people and wheelchair users. The goal is to create places that are not only beautiful but also welcoming to everyone in the community. Inclusive design removes barriers, ensuring everyone has equal comfort and access.

BODIES

· ·

A building won't work for its users if it's the wrong size. Good design helps people complete their daily activities safely and comfortably. Architects make use of something called anthropometry, which comes from the Greek words meaning 'human' and 'measure'. Architects learn the average sizes of the body, furniture and building elements. They use these measurements to make things fit and arrange them in the most convenient way. This means thinking about the details of a building from a user's experience. So if you can easily reach for your toothpaste or work comfortably at your desk, that's thanks to anthropometry!

Villa E-1027

MODERNISM

Modernist architecture, which flourished in the 1920s, was a new way of designing,
inspired by advances in science and technology. Modernist architects preferred simplicity
and industrial features. You can often recognise a modernist building by its plain white exterior,
rectangular shape and long horizontal windows. A classic example is Villa E-1027, in France,
designed in the 1920s by Irish architect Eileen Gray. She was also an exceptional
artist and furniture designer, who created many modern items for the villa that were both
stylish and flexible. She looked to the future in the hope of creating a new way of living.

The Eames House

CHARLES AND RAY EAMES

· ·

Charles and Ray Eames were a married couple who were also design partners. Based in California, their creative partnership flourished for more than thirty years. They designed their own home – a classic example of American modernism with clean lines, tall ceilings and big industrial windows. It's also playful, with the outside featuring bright primary colours. The Eameses loved creating designs together, and their playfulness always shines through. They designed fabrics, art, films and furniture, including many chairs that are still in production today. Their trademark was interesting shapes made from equally interesting materials, such as moulded plastic, fibreglass and plywood.

Nawarla Gabarnmung

CAVE

....

For tens of thousands of years, humans have lived in caves. These natural chambers, or holes, provided shelter from the weather and a safe place for sleeping and cooking. Archaeologists discovered that one Australian cave was occupied for 30,000 years. It's called Nawarla Gabarnmung, meaning 'place of the hole in the rock'. The people who lived there carved into the rock, removing parts of the cave to create a more comfortable shelter. This shows that humans have been adapting their living spaces for a long time. Later people went a step further by decorating their caves with paintings of animals.

COMMUNITY

· ·

A community is all about bringing people together. And architecture is an important part of any community! Buildings can have a positive impact on people's lives, by giving them a place to go and helping them take part in community life. Community centres are buildings that a whole neighbourhood or town can use. They provide useful spaces for people to come together for parties, play groups, classes and meetings. Courtyard designs can be a great way of creating a sense of belonging. The courtyard becomes the heart of the community and a space for people to meet and exchange ideas.

TENT

Humans have been living in tents for more than 40,000 years. For some, a tent is a short-term shelter for camping on holiday; for others, it is home. Tents are strong, they last and are easy to carry. The earliest tents were made from the bones and hides of woolly mammoths. Nomadic Native Americans sometimes used lightweight cone-shaped tepees made of buffalo hide, which were easy to put up and take down. In the Middle East, Bedouin tents made from goat hair keep out the rain and stay cool in summer. Mongolian yurts are round and made of sheep felt.

Pyramids of Giza (Egypt)

The Great Ziggurat of Ur (Iraq)

Chichen Itza Pyramid (Mexico)

PYRAMID

A pyramid is a structure with sloping sides that meet at a single peak at its top. The base of a pyramid can be a square, triangle or another shape. In the ancient Middle East, temples called ziggurats were pyramid-shaped, but their sides were stepped rather than sloping. The Great Pyramid of Giza in Cairo, Egypt, was built in about 2550 BCE, and it was the tallest structure in the world for thousands of years, until the soaring spire of Lincoln Cathedral, England, overtook it. In Mexico, the Maya also built incredible stepped pyramids at sites such as Chichen Itza.

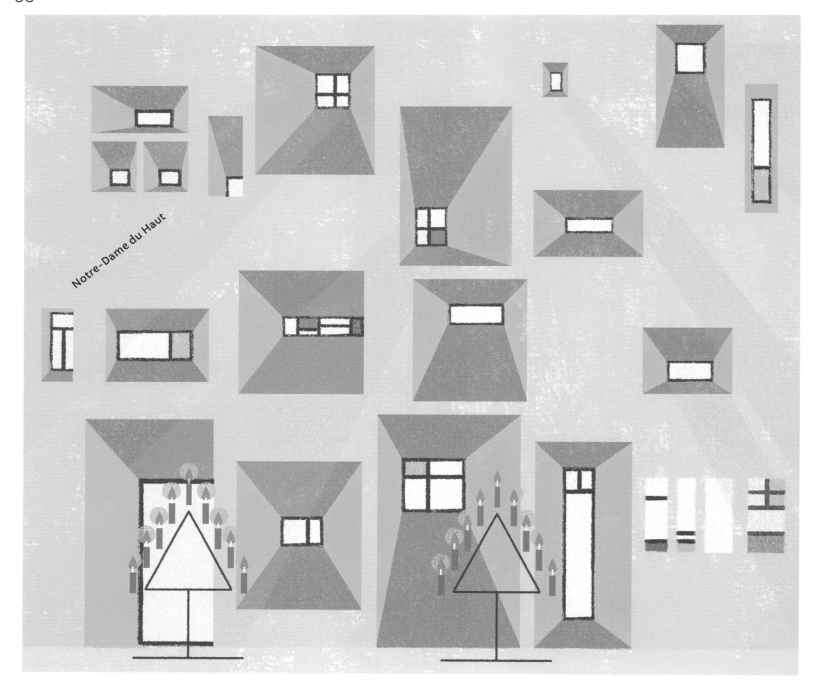

Notre-Dame du Haut

LIGHT

· ·

Light is necessary for life. It's also important for health. Architects think carefully about where a building will sit in relation to the sun – this is called orientation. The orientation of a building is one of the most important decisions an architect can make. Positioning the building to face the sun's path means that it will capture natural light. In the 1950s, architect Le Corbusier used light as a material when designing the Chapel of Notre Dame. Windows of different sizes are cut into the thick walls, capturing the sunlight. The small chapel seems to glow, transformed by magical daylight.

Cliff Face House

SHADE

Now more than ever, humans and buildings need protection from the sun. One simple way to cool a building is to create shade. In his houses in Australia, Peter Stutchbury uses traditional cooling techniques such as large roofs, overhangs and window shades to keep out the sun. Thanks to closely packed buildings and pavements that absorb heat, cities are often hotter than the surrounding areas – this is a condition known as the heat island effect. We can try to reverse this by planting trees along the streets, using light-coloured roofs and choosing building materials to reflect rather than absorb heat.

RIAD

Riad means 'garden' in Arabic. Sometimes spelled 'riyad', the word is used for a Moroccan home arranged around an internal garden. The beauty of the riad is hidden behind tall walls and a simple door that reveal no hint of what's behind. Riads have symmetrical courtyards, which means they are the same on both sides. Sometimes there is a fountain surrounded by trees in the middle. Often a riad is two storeys high, with a rooftop adorned with carved timbers and geometric patterned tiles called *zelij*. The columns along the courtyard are often connected by arches to form a colonnade.

RYOKAN

A ryokan is a traditional Japanese inn, famous for its uniquely Japanese style. Ryokans may be one of the oldest forms of hotel, dating back to the 8th century CE. They have a special place in Japanese traditional culture. Guests change into lightweight *yukata* robes and slippers and sit on mats around low tables to eat delicious meals, using traditional manners. At night the guests sleep on mattresses called futons. Screens called *shoji*, made of bamboo and rice paper, can open up to reveal the world outside. There is often a beautiful Japanese garden that contains rocks and bonsai trees.

Darling Square Library

KENGO KUMA

The architect Kengo Kuma is a master of materials. Each building he creates is a one-off. Kuma uses building materials both for decoration and for building. He experiments and sees each project as an opportunity to push the limits of whatever material he is using. Whether his buildings are made of stone, glass or timber, the material is always the star! The Darling Square Library in Sydney, Australia, expresses the timeless beauty and flexibility of wood. About 20 km of sustainable timber panels create the library's looped, eye-catching curves. Kuma's designs are Japanese in spirit, but they have global appeal.

National Museum of African American History and Culture

SIR DAVID ADJAYE

Sir David Adjaye is an award-winning Ghanaian British architect. As a child, he lived in many different parts of Africa and the Middle East. This nomadic upbringing left him inspired by many different cultures. Now he creates grand, visual building designs which often explore materials and patterns. Adjaye believes that architecture can create powerful emotions. He is influenced by the art of sculpture, which is shown in the National Museum of African American History and Culture in Washington, D.C. The building takes the shape of a layered trapezoid (see page 51) and helps visitors connect with the history and exhibits.

Temple Mount
(Israel)

Amritsar
(India)

St Basil's Cathedral
(Russia)

Boudhanath (Nepal)

PLACE OF WORSHIP

The buildings that worshippers visit to connect with their faith can take many forms, including cathedrals, churches, mosques, pagodas, stupas, synagogues and temples. The design of a building connects to how it will be used. The Buddhist stupa of Boudhanath is a tall mound-shaped structure that worshippers walk around. St Basil's Cathedral in Moscow has colourful onion domes. Muslim mosques face towards the holy city of Mecca. Gold is often used on religious buildings to show how holy they are. Both the Sikh temple of Amritsar in India and the Temple Mount in Jerusalem shine magnificently as symbols of devotion.

Heddal Stave Church

STAVE

A seven-hundred-year-old wooden church stands in Heddal, Norway. It is Norway's largest remaining stave church. These churches have a sturdy timber frame – 'stave' means 'post' in old Norse. The stunning churches are the result of Vikings passing down their craftsmanship and skills. They were built in the Gothic period, which lasted from the 12th to the 16th century. Their design takes inspiration from Gothic churches elsewhere in Europe. The Gothic features of the Heddal church include spires and dragon-shaped gargoyles, which are carved spouts on the roof. The distinctive roofs are steep to ensure that heavy winter snow slides off.

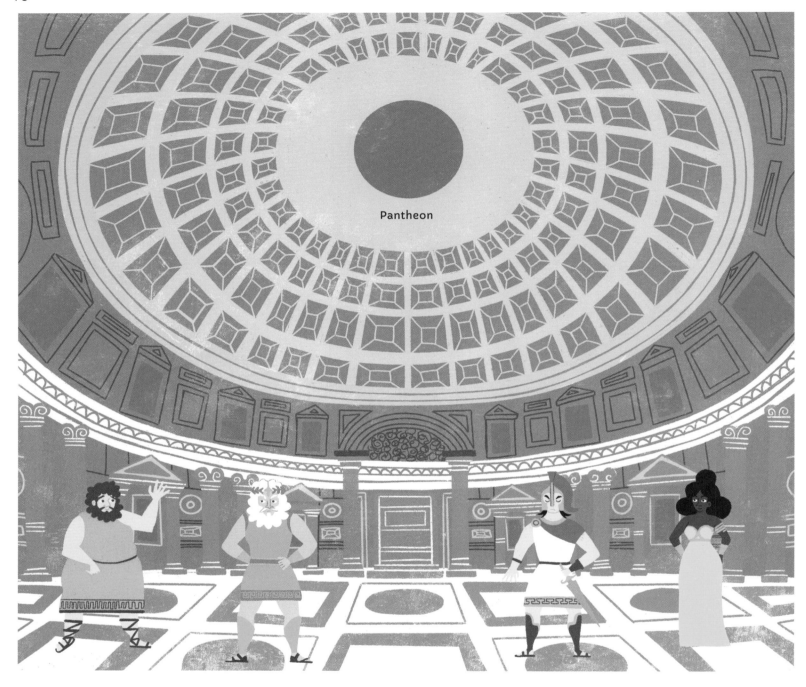

Pantheon

DOME

A dome is a rounded roof on a building. Domes have been used around the world and throughout history, from huts to stone cathedrals. Domes are often created to inspire and impress. The Pantheon in Rome was built around 125 CE for Emperor Hadrian. It is the world's largest dome made from unreinforced concrete. At the top of the dome is a hole called an oculus, measuring nearly 8 m wide. The interior is 43 m in diameter and it is 22 m high. Nearly 2,000 years after its construction, the Pantheon remains an ancient wonder, worthy of a visit.

Reichstag

REICHSTAG

· ·

Since 1894, the Reichstag has been home to the German parliament, where the government meets. The building originally had a dome which was destroyed by fire in 1933. Architect Norman Foster created an exciting new replacement, which was completed in 2004. A mirrored cone bounces light onto parliament members below. Visitors can climb one of two dramatic spiral ramps to visit the dome and either watch the debate or enjoy the view outside. The new Reichstag dome is one of Berlin's most impressive landmarks. It is a futuristic symbol of modern Germany, proving that architecture can help define a nation.

DISASSEMBLY

Disassembly means taking something apart. When architects design a building, they must think about what will happen to it at the end of its useful life. Construction creates a lot of waste. Often building scrap, such as concrete, rock and soil, is sent to landfill, which means it's not recycled. This is not sustainable for the future, so new ideas are needed. Architects are pledging to change this wastefulness by building smarter. In London, architect Janine Campbell is pioneering 'Design for Disassembly' – studying the life cycle of all building parts and creating buildings where everything can be reused and repurposed.

REINVENT

· ·

Anne Lacaton and Jean-Philippe Vassal are award-winning French architects who are committed
to creating affordable buildings that make clever use of materials to avoid any waste. They
are leaders of a movement aimed at creating better homes from buildings that already exist,
without the need for demolishing and rebuilding. Their apartment designs often have large, open
multi-purpose living rooms, and a modern, industrial style. The simple design allows the owners to
add their own personal touches. The apartments often have private balconies that provide
a relaxing space for the occupants to connect with the outdoors, through fresh air and sun.

Beijing National Stadium

STADIUM

A stadium is a large sports ground designed to hold athletes and spectators. They have existed since at least 776 BCE, when the ancient Olympic Games began. For the Beijing Games of 2008, the architecture firm of Herzog & de Meuron teamed up with the Chinese artist Ai Weiwei to create the Beijing National Stadium – affectionally called the 'Bird's Nest' due to the appearance of its complicated design. The stadium can hold 91,000 spectators for sports events or concerts. Bird nests are considered lucky in Chinese culture, making the stadium an impressive building with a design that is uniquely Chinese.

The London Mastaba

TRAPEZOID

A trapezoid is a four-sided shape where two of the sides are parallel, which means the lines are the same distance apart. Architects often use the trapezoid shape in their designs. Christo is an artist and he used a trapezoid shape when designing a mastaba for the Serpentine Gallery in London. A mastaba is a traditional style of Egyptian tomb – an ancient use of a trapezoid shape. To bring his mastaba up to date, Christo made it from bright pink oil barrels, then set it floating on water. The trapezoid rises 20 m high, giving it a powerful, bold presence.

VITRUVIUS

· ·

Marcus Vitruvius Pollio, who lived in the 1st century BCE, was a Roman military engineer and architect. He is better known simply as Vitruvius. He was a great admirer of Greek architecture, and a book that he wrote about architecture remained popular for hundreds of years. In fact, his ideas and illustrations defined what western architecture looked like! Vitruvius believed that architecture is a combination of science, mathematics, geometry, astronomy, medicine, meteorology and philosophy. He thought architects were more than designers – they should have knowledge of art, nature and science. According to Vitruvius, buildings should be stable, useful and beautiful.

SKETCH

A sketch is a loose drawing, often done quickly. It is a way of expressing ideas and communicating with others. Instead of communicating through words or numbers, architects share their vision through sketch drawings. In fact, architects think by drawing. Making sketches often helps spark their creativity. The Italian architect Aldo Rossi drew expressively, using watercolours and ink, and his drawings became artworks in themselves. Like many architects, Rossi used sketching as a vital part of his creative process. A simple sketch created with a pencil is more expressive than a line generated by a computer. Give it a go!

Colosseum

Saint Peter's Basilica

Aqueduct
of Segovia

ROMAN

The Roman Empire spanned three continents, uniting parts of Europe, Asia and Africa.
Roman influence can still be seen in science and government – and in architecture too.
The Romans were excellent builders, engineers and architects. As they spread out from their
capital city of Rome, they built water systems, called aqueducts, and roads. They developed
the use of arches and domes. They were such amazing builders that many of their buildings, roads
and settlements are still standing. Examples include the Colosseum and the Pantheon in Rome,
various aqueducts and the Appian Way, which is one of the first superhighways constructed.

Parthenon

ANCIENT GREEK

Ancient Greek temples are well-known for their beauty and sense of order. Many temples still exist and the most famous is the majestic Temple of Athena, better known as the Parthenon. It was built between 447 and 438 BCE to honour Athena, patron goddess of Athens. Perched high on a hill called the Acropolis, the Parthenon has 69 fluted columns arranged in two ranks. The triangular top, called a pediment, was painted gold, red and blue, and decorated with sculptures. For centuries, architects have copied this style. You may be able to spot these features on churches and town halls.

Antares Tower (Barcelona)

Exhibition Information Centre
(China)

ODILE DECQ

Odile Decq is a French architect and teacher who looks more like a punk rock star
than an architect. Her designs are not quiet and polite – they are dramatic and vivid. Red
is a passionate colour and it has become her signature. The red objects in her buildings
often create surprising experiences. When Decq begins planning a building, she always
thinks of how her body will experience the space, hoping to express movement in her
designs. She created an architecture school called Confluence to inspire future architects
and share her love of architecture. She believes architecture can change the world.

EXPERIMENTAL

Archigram was a group of experimental architects based in London. In the early 1960s they published a magazine to share their ideas, which were devoted to experimental new designs and ways of living. The magazine was full of bold structures inspired by cartoons. The Archigram architects were influenced by pop culture, technology and science fiction. They drew over 900 designs, such as walking cities, space capsules and cities made of balloons! The group even created a 'plug-in city', where machines placed capsule homes on to a high-rise megastructure. Today, Archigram's ideas are still as experimental – and as inspirational – as ever.

LESS

· ·

Yasmeen Lari, Pakistan's first female licensed architect, calls herself a barefoot architect. She feels that while architecture should tread lightly on the natural surroundings, it is also a powerful tool for encouraging communities to live better lives. Lari believes that everyone – whether they are rich or poor – should experience good design. She focuses on creating shelter for the poor, working with local villagers and craftspeople to build wonderful designs with less. Lari believes that we can create a more sustainable future with new simple designs. She is a champion of quality design, made from basic materials and accessible to all.

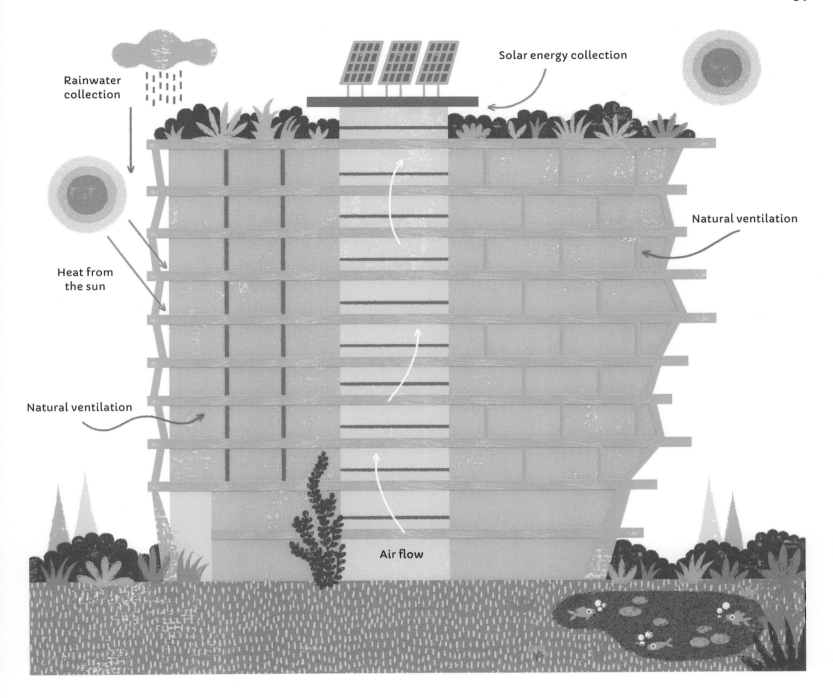

Rainwater collection

Solar energy collection

Natural ventilation

Heat from the sun

Natural ventilation

Air flow

ENERGY

More than forty per cent of the energy used around the world is used in homes and other buildings. To reduce energy use, our buildings must become more energy-efficient and sustainable. Everyone can make small savings by switching to LED lights, installing energy-efficient appliances, hanging washing outside, unplugging appliances when not using them and sealing gaps to stop leaks. But designing buildings well can save more energy. This might mean using natural ventilation (windows and doors) to heat and cool our buildings, designing them so they generate their own renewable electricity and making use of solar energy to heat water.

Shibam

HEIGHT

In the middle of the desert in Yemen, a tall mud-brick city stands alongside a
dried-up river bed. This enchanting metropolis, called Shibam, is often referred to as 'the
Manhattan of the Desert', thanks to its resemblance to the skyscrapers of New York City.
About 500 mud-brick towers rise upwards, packed tightly together – standing between five
and eleven storeys high. Most of the buildings are over 500 years old, making it the world's
oldest high-rise city. Shibam was an important stop on the spice-trading routes,
and the height of the city helped protect the residents from attacks from rival tribes.

Great Mosque of Djenné

MUD BRICK

The Great Mosque of Djenné in Mali is the largest mud-brick structure in the world. The current version of the mosque was built in 1907. The thick walls are made of mud bricks finished with a layer of clay. There are many bundles of palm branches sticking out from the walls. These sticks are part of the mosque's decoration, but they also have an important function. Rain wears away the mud bricks, so the building needs frequent repairs, when the sticks are used as scaffolding. Replastering the Great Mosque has become an annual festival – and a celebration for the community.

Palais Bulles

BUBBLE PALACE

· ·

In the 1970s, Antti Lovag created an imaginative house in the South of France. He called it Palais Bulles, which means 'bubble palace'! The design is an extraordinary mixture of intersecting domes that look like giant bubbles. It was so complex that the building took fourteen years to complete. The property's owners have said that its curves and softness create a feel-good atmosphere. Lovag much preferred curves over straight lines, so everything in the house is round – even the doors and windows. The home is somewhere between a futuristic cave and a fantasy bubble city. In a word, it's bubble-icious!

The 'House of Bread'

BLOB ARCHITECTURE

· ·

The invention of computer-aided design software, known as CAD, allowed architects more freedom with their imaginations. Since the 1990s, architects such as Wolf Prix and a firm called Future Systems have used CAD to create bold, futuristic designs inspired by nature and science. These architects found inspiration in curved, natural shapes, such as water droplets and sea creatures. Their designs have no straight edges, are often uniquely shaped, and are made of unusual metal tiles or peculiar materials. Keep looking out for blobs – you will see them in graphic design, artwork and the occasional building. Blob architecture has wow factor!

Blur Building

LIGHTNESS

In the past buildings were made of stone. Heavy stone needs thick walls for maximum support, giving buildings a weighty appearance. But as technology has improved, architects have been pushing the boundaries of materials so they can make buildings light, not heavy. The Blur Building was created on a lake in Switzerland for an exhibition in 2002. It included 35,000 nozzles that sprayed water to create a haze of white mist. Visitors stood in a misty environment and felt like they were floating in the air. At the same time, the building seemed to disappear, becoming nothing more than fog.

SkyPark

CANTILEVER

· ·

Architects love to trick the eye using clever structural elements to make a heavy building look light. They often use cantilevers to achieve this effect. A cantilever is a structure that extends out horizontally, so from side to side, supported at only one end. Roofs and balconies often make use of cantilevers. The world's longest public cantilever, called SkyPark, is in Singapore. High above the ground, it spans three 55-storey hotel towers, stretching as long as four aeroplanes laid end-to-end. The SkyPark includes gardens, restaurants and an infinity pool. And what holds up Singapore's boldest icon? A cantilever, of course!

Bamboo
building

BAMBOO

Bamboo is one of the world's fastest growing plants. It is remarkably tough – it can stand squashing pressures better than steel can! Treated bamboo can be very durable. It can also be bent to make beautiful curves and shapes. In Bali and Vietnam, architects are using bamboo to create impressive natural buildings. The way that the bamboo is shaped makes the buildings look fantastical, like somewhere that a hobbit might live! The bamboo makes the buildings look like part of the natural environment. The bamboo homes designed by the Canadian designer Elora Hardy in Bali are completely natural and magical.

Fungus Among Us

NATURE

· ·

When it comes to design, nature is the ultimate inspiration. Today, architects are incorporating nature into more designs. Biophilic means 'loving life', and biophilic design aims to create opportunities to connect with nature in our daily lives, through the spaces where we spend most of our time. Biophilic designers use water, natural light, fresh air and living plants to create appealing spaces. They take visual inspiration from trees, mushrooms, shells, waterfalls and animals to create interesting new forms and shapes. As we spend more time in indoor spaces, opportunities to get closer to nature are more crucial than ever before.

PLAN

An architectural plan is a drawing that shows a building's layout and structure as if viewed from above. A floor plan usually displays all of a building's elements as if they are at a height of one metre, so that means windows are included. Floor plans are the basis of all other architectural drawings. Looking at a plan can be strange at first as they are a type of visual language that takes practice to master. Architects all follow the same rules when drawing plans, so once the symbols and styles have been learnt, reading a plan becomes really straightforward.

Federation Square

FRACTALS

· ·

A fractal is a type of pattern that repeats itself over and over in smaller sizes. Fractals are often found in nature, such as in the branching arms of a snowflake or the intricate fronds of a fern. In their design for Federation Square in Melbourne, Australia, LAB Architects used fractals as their inspiration. The glass atrium, or hall, of the cultural centre looks like smashed glass or ice crystals. LAB hoped to inspire the public with mathematics while creating something daring. Federation Square is a symbol of Melbourne's creativity and serves to show how amazing public buildings can be.

Honeycomb Apartments

SOCIAL

Public housing – also known as social housing – are homes provided by a government authority. Housing can be expensive, but the United Nations states that access to a fair standard of living is a basic human right. Children in particular need housing to feel safe and protected. Many architects are passionate about creating social housing that is attractive and well designed, as well as affordable for all. In Slovenia, one innovative social housing development was designed to provide homes for low-income families. Inspired by the shape of a honeycomb, the apartments' eye-catching pop-out balconies make the community look fun and exciting.

Royal Ontario Museum

DECONSTRUCTIVISM

· ·

Deconstructivist designs first appeared in the 1980s. They were brand new and thought-provoking, as architects tried to take apart their designs to create something powerful and unusual. The designs didn't rely on traditional square or rectangular shapes. Instead, the buildings were made up of sharp-angled shapes that smashed into each other, giving the appearance of chaos. In his designs, Daniel Libeskind creates feeling and movement with sharp lines and angles. Some of his buildings look like giant crystals. For an extension to the Royal Ontario Museum in Canada, Libeskind created a bold, metallic jewel-like form that appears to crash into the existing building.

CCTV Headquarters

INVENTIVE

· ·

Being inventive means thinking originally to create new things. In architecture, this can range from creating new shapes to using new materials. In his design for the CCTV Headquarters building in Beijing, Dutch architect Rem Koolhaas increased the floor space not by going taller, but by creating a looped shape. The inventive and unusual design is made from two leaning towers angled at ninety degrees. It includes a 75-metre-long cantilever called the 'Overhang', suspended high above the ground. This remarkable building's design was so inventive that it took ten years to construct. The architects managed to make the impossible possible.

Upside-down House
(Germany)

Strawberry House
(Brazil)

Kindergarten Wolfartsweier
(Germany)

NOVELTY

Novelty architecture is sometimes known as mimetic architecture. This word comes from mimicry, meaning copying. This form of design was popular at 1950s road stops in the USA, with buildings that look like supersized objects, such as animals and food items. Critics often dismiss these designs as kitsch or ugly, but novelty designs connect with their audience and create delight. Around the world there are buildings that look like strawberries or upside-down houses. A nursery built recently in Germany was designed to look like a cat. At the rear, a slide forms the cat's tail. The design is pure purr-fection!

St Basil's Cathedral

DECORATION

· ·

In architecture, ornament is an element added to a structure, usually for decoration. Architects can choose to show local culture in buildings and adding ornamentation can be a way of telling stories, creating visual interest and celebrating the skills of local craftspeople. St Basil's Cathedral, in Moscow, Russia, is an exceptional example of decoration. Built in 1555–1561, the cathedral has nine onion-shaped domes. Blue, green and red domes with striped patterns define the elaborate roofs. Grouped together on the building, they make it look like the flames of a fire. Colour, pattern and ornament in design create visual joy!

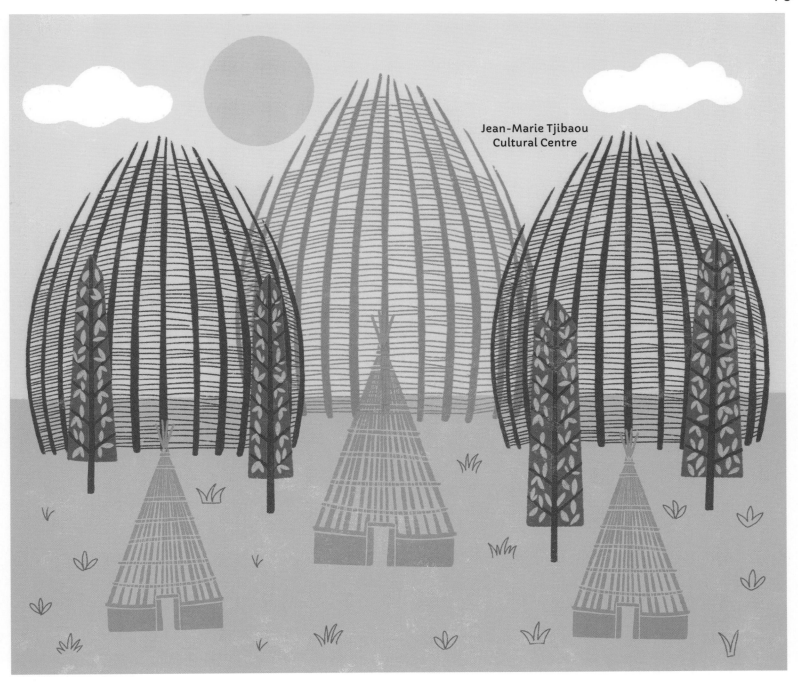

Jean-Marie Tjibaou
Cultural Centre

CULTURE

· ·

Architects often draw inspiration from the local area's traditional forms, then think about them again in a new way. By considering the local landscape and style, architects can design modern buildings that fit in with the site's surroundings and culture. In the territory of New Caledonia, located in the South Pacific, the Jean-Marie Tjibaou Cultural Centre showcases the indigenous Kanak culture. In his design for the building, the Italian architect Renzo Piano took inspiration from the island's traditional architecture. The building's rounded, airy shells were inspired by cone-shaped wooden huts. Their layout is similar to that of a Kanak village.

West Kowloon Station

STATION

Train stations have long been a feature of town and city landscapes. In fact, the first train station – in Swansea, Wales – opened in 1807 and it's carriages were originally horse-drawn. Over 200 years later, West Kowloon Station was built to connect Hong Kong to mainland China by high-speed rail. Andrew Bromberg's design for the building seems to grow from the ground and reflects the speed and movement of trains. The soaring glass walls and roof of the arrival hall greet arriving passengers with a view of Hong Kong's famous skyline. The station's gravity-defying futuristic design is a celebration of travel.

Arch of Septimius Severus

ARCH

Arches are strong, curved structures that are used to carry weight – usually spanning a gap or opening. An arch has a purpose – it holds things up – but it can also be decorative. The ancient Romans often incorporated grand arches into their designs for buildings and bridges, many of which are still standing today. In Palmyra, Syria, Romans created this triumphal arch. The Monumental Arch, also called the Arch of Septimius Severus, was a decorative archway of great beauty. It was Palmyra's main tourist attraction until it was destroyed in 2015. There are plans to rebuild it using the original stone.

Burdei hut

HUT

· ·

Huts are a traditional form of shelter, made from accessible, sturdy materials such as mud, straw, wood, bones or bricks. Huts can be found across the world. Huts are sometimes round or have triangular sloped sides, because these designs are strong but easily constructed. Traditional huts are often created using building techniques passed down through the generations. For example, burdei are hut-based structures that look like log cabins. The architectural style is from the Carpathian Mountains of Eastern Europe and has been passed down through generations and from around the world, with the earliest Ukrainian Canadian settlers constructing similar houses.

Tulou

TULOU

....

Tulou are circular or square buildings found in the Fujian province of southeastern China. The name means 'earthen building', thanks to their mixture of thick clay and wood walls. A tulou has one entrance leading to a central courtyard and is often three or more storeys high. Some of these buildings can house up to 800 people, making them a wonderful example of communal living. Children who live in a tulou will often eat at a neighbour's house, while their parents go to work. The O shape encourages the residents to come together in the courtyard for festivals and events.

Inujima Art House Project

KAZUYO SEJIMA

· ·

The Japanese architect Kazuyo Sejima is the second woman to receive the Pritzker Prize.
SANAA, the architecture company she co-founded, is recognised for its playful and relaxed
approach to design. Sejima's inventive style means that her designs are always unique and
stylish. She tries to bring lightness and brightness into her structures, which makes them
appear modern, and as if you could blink and they'd be gone. At the Inujima Art House,
on a small Japanese island, Sejima created a see-through circular pavilion. Visitors can
walk amongst its brightly coloured flowers and look through it, out on to the village.

Louvre Museum

TRANSPARENCY

When something is transparent you can see through it. Architects often try to make heavy objects look light using transparency. Windows and glass walls bring light and a feeling of space into a building. The inside and outside are connected visually, even if they're physically separated. At Paris's Louvre Museum, I M Pei created a spectacular glass pyramid, similar to the Pyramid of Giza in Egypt. The glass pyramid is 22 m high and contains 673 panes of extra-clear laminated glass. It is the entry to the world's most visited museum, an impressive landmark of Paris and of modern-day architecture.

Centre Pompidou

HIGH-TECH

· ·

The high-tech movement in architecture, which began in the 1970s, was an exciting time. Buildings became bold and mechanical-looking forms that showed off their structure instead of hiding it. The structure became the building's decoration. Even a building's pipes, stairs and mechanical systems became decorative features. Materials such as plastic and metal replaced stone and other traditional materials, giving buildings a futuristic appearance. Two young architects, Richard Rogers and Renzo Piano, created the Centre Pompidou in Paris. It's an inside-out project, where the mechanics are on proud display – a colourful machine for living and a one-of-a-kind masterpiece. J'adore le Pompidou!

Geisel Library

BRUTALISM

· ·

Brutalism is a controversial style – people either love or hate its use of concrete and strong, zigzag shapes. Starting in about 1950, many architects chose to create enormous designs in concrete. The Geisel Library in La Jolla, California, was built in 1970 to a design by William Pereira. The library's iconic stepped shape can be viewed from any angle. It shines like a diamond or crystal, and also appears light, despite its size and weight. Love it or hate it, brutalism was a creative period in the history of architecture. The world's brutalist buildings should be admired for their design.

Princess Elisabeth Antarctica

EXTREME

Did you know that no humans live permanently in Antarctica? Antarctica is the coldest and most isolated place on Earth, but it's the ideal location for scientific studies, such as research on climate change and rising sea levels. There are dozens of scientific bases in Antarctica, with over 4,000 people living there during the summer. One base, the Princess Elisabeth, is the first energy-efficient research station. This means it uses exactly as much energy as is needed, without waste. For example, the station doesn't use heating – it uses electrical equipment and the scientists' own bodies to keep the building warm!

WaterNest

OFF-GRID

· ·

When a building is off-grid, it is not connected to local supplies of water and electricity or systems to take waste away. Instead, an off-grid building must be self-sufficient. It often has systems for collecting rainwater, plus solar panels for generating electricity. New technology has made off-grid homes easier to build. Off-grid living isn't something that only happens in remote areas, now many new inner-city projects are creating off-grid homes. They look normal but can generate their own electricity. Italian architect Giancarlo Zema has designed an eco-friendly floating home called WaterNest, where occupants can live in peaceful harmony with nature.

Angkor Wat

ANGKOR WAT

· ·

Angkor Wat is a jaw-dropping series of monuments built in the 12th century. Near the Cambodian city of Siem Reap, it is a place of wonder and majesty. But although it is the world's largest religious set of buildings, it was forgotten about for centuries, hidden deep in the jungle. Angkor Wat covers 160 hectares, so it would take over a week to explore it properly. There are over one thousand buildings and dozens of temples, each one more magnificent than the next! Many of them sit inside a moat. The temples hold sculptures of dancing women and large Buddhas.

Old Bagan

PAGODA

A pagoda is a tall, tiered structure that has religious significance. Pagodas have an array of different shaped roofs depending on the region where they are built. The ancient city of Bagan, in Myanmar, is a fascinating place to see pagodas. From the 11th century to the 13th century, Bagan was the capital of the Pagan Empire. There are more than 3,000 temples, pagodas and monasteries located on its plains. The local Buddhist people built these red brick pagodas as a way of showing their devotion. You can take a balloon ride and experience the amazing buildings from up high!

Santa Marta Favela

FAVELA

In Brazil, a favela is a settlement or neighbourhood where people have built their homes, without help from the government. Favelas are often crowded and lacking in facilities. Today around 12 million people live in favelas across Brazil, including nearly 25 per cent of the population of Rio de Janeiro. Many favela homes are at risk from flooding and landslides, due to their unstable position on steep mountainsides. But favelas have a positive side too. Artists and community members have improved their homes with brightly coloured murals and beautiful mosaics. They show pride in their homes and in their communities.

Paper log house

HUMANITY

· ·

Around the world, about 60 million people do not have basic shelter, which means they do not have a place to live. They are in need of humanitarian aid. Solving this problem can be life-changing for struggling families. Luckily, there are humanitarian projects which provide design and building services to communities affected by disasters. Being a humanitarian means helping others in need. Architects can do this by using their creativity to help the people who need it most. Japanese architect Shigeru Ban is an example of humanitarianism. He creates affordable homes and churches out of paper tubes and recycled materials.

MINECRAFT

Created in Sweden, Minecraft is the world's best-selling video game. It has over 140 million regular users, who use virtual building blocks to create structures. First released in 2011, it quickly became a global sensation. Minecraft encourages users to explore their imagination, using different types of blocks to create whatever they desire. It's an unlimited digital world, full of possibilities and easy to lose yourself in. In the game's creative mode, users choose blocks and build whatever they want. You can learn spatial awareness, geometry, teamwork and creativity. Minecraft is training the next generation of designers, which is very exciting!

The Farmhouse (model)

M O D U L A R

Our cities are growing, but we need them to grow efficiently and sustainably. In the future timber skyscrapers or 'plyscrapers' could become the new norm because they are kinder to the environment. Using a modular design will make high-rises easier and faster to build. A modular building is made up of smaller identical parts, or modules. They are often premade and then assembled on-site. Architects Chris and Fei Precht have designed a timber skyscraper, where the timber is stacked in triangular panels. Residents will be encouraged to grow plants and food in the gaps between modules, creating a sky-high farmhouse!

Sharp Centre for Design

SCALE

. . . .

In architecture, scale refers to the relative visual size of something – that is, how big it looks next to something else. Architects often draw their building plans at 1:100, meaning that every centimetre on the plan corresponds to 100 cm in real life when the house is built. At the Sharp Centre for Design in Toronto, Canada, the architect Will Alsop played with scale by creating a new building towering over an existing one. The sight of a large soaring rectangle hovering eight storeys above the ground creates tension. Visitors who experience this remarkable and brave design find it breathtaking.

Nature Boardwalk,
Lincoln Park Zoo

JEANNE GANG

Founded by architect Jeanne Gang, Studio Gang is a firm that creates exciting and forward-thinking designs. Gang believes that an architect's job is to design relationships, because cities are all about places where people come together. Studio Gang has been working with local government to make buildings more bird-friendly. One of their projects was revitalizing an area of Lincoln Park Zoo, Chicago, by building a boardwalk through the lakeside ecosystem. It includes an outdoor classroom pavilion, or garden shelter, made of lightweight premade sections that the builders were able to install by hand. It provides a space for connecting and learning about nature.

Hawa Mahal

MUGHAL

Mughal architecture is an Indian building style created by Mughal rulers in the mid-1500s. Inspired by the Islamic architecture of Turkey and Persia, Mughal buildings are full of geometric shapes and beautiful decoration. The city of Jaipur, India, is home to the Hawa Mahal. Made of startlingly pink sandstone, the building – nicknamed the Palace of the Winds – was built in 1799 by Maharaja Sawai. It stands five storeys tall, with over 950 intricate bay windows called *jharokhas* that give the building a honeycomb appearance. From these windows, the royal women could watch the world go by on the street below.

Neuschwanstein Castle

CASTLE

Castles capture the imagination like few other types of buildings. They are huge with interesting shapes not often seen on modern buildings, such as tall towers, ornamental turrets and patterns. As the homes of royal families, castles provide the backdrop for many fairy tales. Neuschwanstein Castle in Germany looks like something out of a dream, but it's very real – it was built for King Ludwig II of Bavaria in the 1800s. Its tall turrets and rugged hilltop setting make it look romantic and dramatic. The castle shows how architecture can create fantasy and mystery though its unusual shapes and structures.

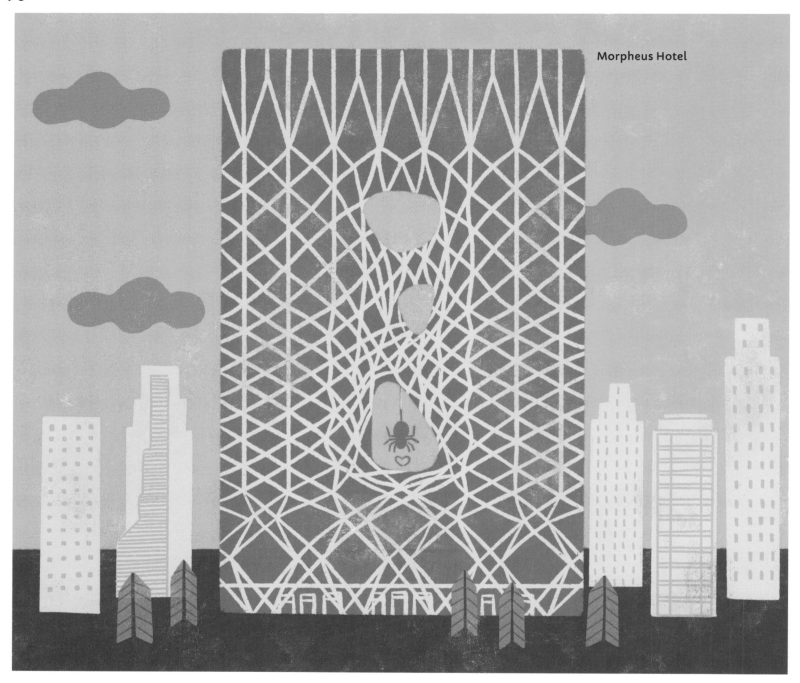

Morpheus Hotel

EXOSKELETON

· ·

An exoskeleton is the hard outer shell found in some invertebrate animals, such as cicadas, ladybirds, lobsters and crabs. The external skeleton supports and protects the body of invertebrates. In architecture, a building's structure can also be highlighted on the outside, forming an exoskeleton that is both decorative and structural. Morpheus Hotel in Macau, designed by Dame Zaha Hadid, may be the world's first exoskeleton high-rise. The external frame is made up of 2,500 steelwork connections. The exoskeleton gives the hotel a funky, futuristic look, but it is also strong and highly functional. A stay there is an extraordinary experience!

Petersen Automotive Museum

FAÇADE

. . . .

The word 'façade' is an architectural term for describing the main outside wall of a building. And getting a building's façade right is so important that these designs have become a specialised area of architecture. Façades have an impact on a building's energy efficiency, and they also become part of the streetscape for passers-by to see. When designing a façade, an architect can be creative and use the outside to express the building's use, while considering the local climate, sun, wind and engineering. At the Petersen Automotive Museum in Los Angeles, the red and silver ribbons create a striking façade.

SMART

· ·

Technology is getting smarter every day. In Singapore, a new digital health system includes wearable devices that monitor health and notify the hospital if someone falls and injures themselves. A city's streetscape and architecture can be smart, too! In Zurich, Switzerland, sensors on streetlights monitor traffic levels and automatically turn the lights off when they are not needed. In Oslo, Norway, all new cars will be electric by 2025. Singapore is going a step further, by building a city that will be vehicle-free. As transport creates half of a city's air pollution, this change will lead to better air quality.

CAPSULE

A capsule is a small case or container that's often round or cylindrical in shape. Capsule designs, which are small and self-contained, are useful when there isn't much space. In a capsule hotel – also called a pod hotel – the guest occupies a bed-sized pod that can be closed off with either a door or a curtain. The capsules are arranged in rows and often double-stacked, providing basic but affordable accommodation. The first capsule hotel was built in Japan in 1979, but these designs are now becoming more popular. They can be built quickly and cheaply. They also look really cool.

Taj Mahal

SYMMETRY

A mirror image is symmetrical because it is the same on both sides. Did you know that a butterfly is symmetrical? And humans are hard-wired to find symmetry visually pleasing. Studies show that people judge symmetrical faces to be more attractive, and most people find symmetrical buildings beautiful too. Architects throughout history have used symmetry to create a sense of balance and visual harmony. The Mughal emperor Shah Jahan chose to make the Taj Mahal in India perfectly symmetrical, as a symbol of his love. Many people believe it is the most beautiful building in the world. Do you agree?

GEOMETRIC

· ·

Geometry is an ancient branch of mathematics that deals with points, lines, angles and surfaces. Architects often make use of geometry when they design buildings. An architect might choose a single shape or combine many different shapes together. Buckminster Fuller was an inventor as well as a forward-thinking architect. In 1947, he created the geodesic dome, made up of identical triangles. He worked out the structure by drawing lines on his salad bowls! As he drew these lines, he ended up with a visually interesting structure that was also strong and lightweight. He thought geodesic domes would make brilliant homes.

Rietveld-Schröder House

DE STIJL

De Stijl, which means 'the style', was an art movement founded in the Netherlands in the early 20th century. The movement's artists drew inspiration from vertical (up and down) and horizontal (side to side) lines, and they used only black, white and primary colours. Nothing else in the art world looks quite like De Stijl. The ground-breaking painter Piet Mondrian was one of the movement's founders. The magnificent Rietveld-Schröder House in Utrecht, designed by Gerrit Rietveld, was built in 1924. The building is just like a three-dimensional De Stijl painting! It's a glorious collection of colours, lines and white space.

TEAM

· ·

In architecture, teamwork is an essential skill. You can't expect quality results without good communication. When two or more people or organisations work alongside each other to complete a task or achieve a goal, that's collaboration. Sharing ideas and feedback means that a team can achieve more than one person working on their own. Most collaboration requires leadership, although the form of leadership can be social and friendly. Yvonne Farrell and Shelley McNamara of Grafton Architects were awarded the Pritzker Prize in 2020. They have been collaborating since 1978. Their success proves that a happy partnership can create great architecture.

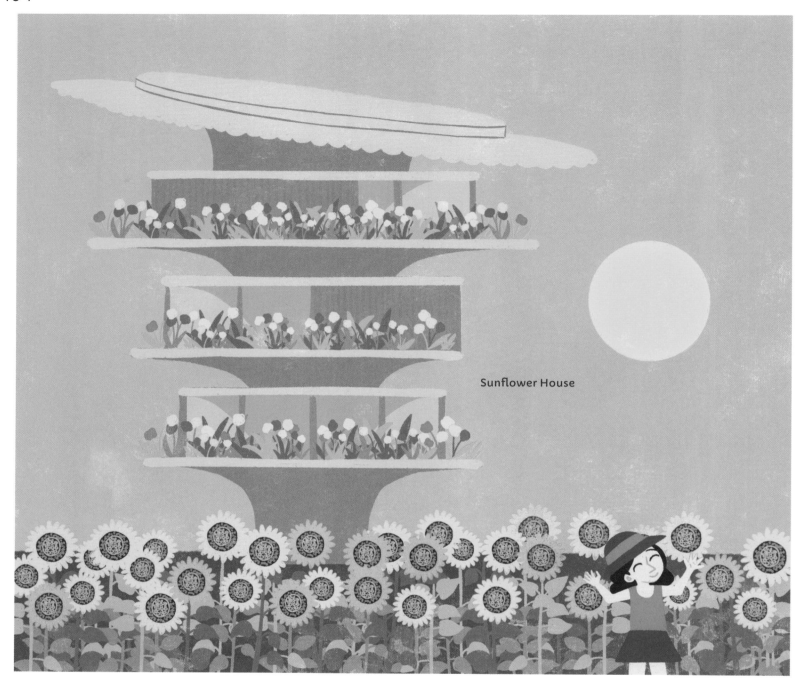

Sunflower House

POSITIVE

Human activity is having a negative effect on Earth's climate, so we need to start making healthier climate choices. A carbon-neutral building produces as much energy as it uses. Architects are now taking this a step further and designing carbon-positive buildings, which produce more energy than they use. Some of these imaginative designs are inspired by a connection to nature. Koichi Takada has designed an innovative home called the Sunflower House. Its stem allows the building to turn so that its solar panels collect as much sunlight as possible. Carbon-positive buildings are a way of helping to reduce our impact.

The High Line

REPURPOSE

To repurpose something means to use it for a different purpose. Architects use the term 'adaptive reuse' to mean finding new life for old buildings or spaces. For example, a tram shed can be turned into a shopping centre, or a factory into an arts centre. Repurposing is a great way of saving resources and avoiding any waste. The High Line in New York City is an example of adapted reuse. The firm of Diller Scofidio + Renfro created a raised public park on an abandoned railway line. It has been so successful that it has revitalized an entire neighbourhood.

SPACE

Humans are curious beings and space has always captured our imaginations. So far only robotic rovers have visited the surface of Mars, but we hope to one day send astronauts to build settlements there. And architects are already designing research stations! To help people survive on this harsh, unfriendly planet, clever designs are needed. Researchers at NASA are exploring inflatable homes and domes made from the planet's ice. Others are suggesting the use of 3D printed structures. The future looks exciting! But living on Earth is also really amazing, so we first need to look after our own extraordinary planet.

CITY

· ·

By 2050 the world's population will probably be close to ten billion people – and more than 70 per cent of those people will live in cities! Many cities will double in size. Cities in the future will need to be connected, with the same opportunities and access for all. Over the next few years, building designs will change to look and be more sustainable. Public transport will improve and food will be grown in high-rise buildings. Zero-carbon cities may be built in forests and oceans. How architects shape the cities of the future will determine how most humans will live.

AUTHOR'S NOTE

Thank you for joining me in sharing the story of architecture.

Architecture is all around us and it's a record of humankind's endeavours through the centuries. It's also one of the marks we've made on this fragile planet. Understanding architecture better helps us understand ourselves, our shared history and how we can connect with others. Through architecture, creative thinkers can design environments that help everyone share a more eco-friendly, fair and healthy world.

Over the coming years, we will continue to learn from indigenous peoples, the people that originally lived in a country, how to better care for the land. I believe that in the future, readers will use their creativity to make their homes, cities and communities into places of great joy and beauty.

Louise O'Brien

THE FUTURE IS ECO AND IT STARTS NOW!

The Maori people of New Zealand have the word *kaitiakitanga,* which means protecting and securing the future, and respecting their ancestors. Planet Earth deserves buildings that connect with nature. The architects of the future must create intelligent, ecological buildings that respond to climate change. Here are five architects who are creating this greener, happier future.

POD PLAYGROUND

To have a healthy, happy community we need healthy and happy children. By 2030, sixty per cent of all city-dwellers will be aged under 18! TCL landscape architects in Canberra, Australia, created a magical adventureland of super-sized acorn and banksia seed pods. The hope is to inspire children through play to protect nature.

PLANT PAVILION

Diébédo Francis Kéré is an architect who creates designs inspired by Indigenous building traditions. Kere uses architecture to imagine a fairer world. In Montana, USA, Kéré created a shelter built with wood from unhealthy trees. The pavilion's name and inspiration is 'Xylem', which is the name for the tissue that brings water and nutrients to a plant's leaves. The natural form encourages visitors to relax and connect with nature.

FLOATING CITIES

Vincent Callebaut is a Belgian-born 'archibiotect' whose vision of architecture is full of awe-inspiring nature-focused creations. He has created many designs for floating cities that are influenced by sea life. One city is inspired by glowing jellyfish and another is inspired by giant lilypads. When we build new ecological cities in the future, they should link with nature and be uplifting just like Callebaut's designs.

DESERT STAY

Nature is an incredibly intelligent builder. Architects are often inspired by nature, from termite mounds to coral reefs, waterfalls, butterflies, birds and sea life. In the desert of Abu Dhabi (UAE), Aidia Studio created a hotel room based on a seed pod. The façade has a moving screen that opens and closes to provide shade from the extreme temperatures, just like a desert plant.

LAGOON SCHOOL

The Makoko Floating School in Nigeria is at the prototype stage, which means it has not been built yet. It responds to the problem of rising sea levels. Designed by architect Kunlé Adeyemi, the timber pontoons, which are floating structures, can give children a place to learn and thrive. Adeyemi has used simple construction methods that are low-tech and recyclable. It's one cool school!

GLOSSARY

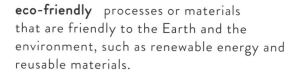

3D 3D stands for three-dimensional. Three-dimensional means you can see something's height, length and width, and it is solid rather than flat (2D).

atrium a tall open space that provides light and air.

biophilic being inspired by the systems found in nature and living things, such as termite mounds, trees and mushrooms. Biophilic designs may become the main building style in the future.

CAD computer-aided design software, which helps architects create their designs. This is one of many software packages available to help designers plan in 3D.

carbon-positive this means that a building or project doesn't only remove as much carbon dioxide from the environment as it produces, it removes more. The result is less carbon dioxide overall.

climate the weather conditions in an area over a long period of time.

colonnade a long external corridor with columns.

composition the way that elements are put together to create something that can be viewed such as an artwork, wall or façade.

cutting-edge forward-thinking design that is new and highly advanced.

durable something that will last a long time.

eco-friendly processes or materials that are friendly to the Earth and the environment, such as renewable energy and reusable materials.

ecological relationship between plants, animals, people and the environment.

ecosystem a community of plants and animals, as well as the environment where they live.

empowering feeling strong or capable.

energy-efficient using exactly as much energy as is needed without wasting any.

façade the main outside wall of a building.

futuristic very modern technology or design that looks like a vision of what is to come in the future.

harmonious/harmony harmonious design is calming to look at because all the parts fit well together.

humanitarian aid being a humanitarian means promoting the rights and wellbeing of humans. Humanitarian aid is therefore giving help to those who need it.

human rights rights all people should have regardless of their race, sex, nationality, religion, language, ethnicity or any other circumstance.

iconic an iconic building is widely known and recognised for its historical, cultural or creative significance.

innovation   the creation of new ideas, styles or ways of doing things.

kitsch   a design that may be considered bad taste because it is over the top.

metropolis   a very large, busy city.

nomadic   people who regularly move from place to place during the year, traditionally with the seasons or for finding food.

organic   curved and flowing.

ornamental   another word for decoration, something that is interesting to look at.

overhang   the part that sticks out over and above something else.

parametricism   a computer-based style of architecture that focuses on curves and irregular shapes.

parliament   a building where elected representatives come to meet to govern a country.

pixels   small units that make up a photo. Some architects have been inspired by them.

pop culture   type of culture, including music, film and television, that is popular with a large number of people.

Pritzker Prize   the prize awarded each year to an architect for their outstanding contribution to architecture.

renewable electricity/energy   power from sources that will not be used up, such as wind, water and the Sun. Wind turbines and solar panels are used to collect renewable energy.

revitalize   in the context of architecture, developing a place or building so that it will look better and become successful again.

scaffolding   place for builders to stand on while they are working on the outside of a building.

streetscape   a view of a street and its environment.

sustainable   something can be used in a way that means it will still be available to use in the future. Sustainable designs are good for the planet.

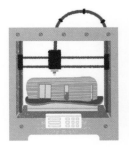

trademark   characteristic of or commonly linked with a particular person or style.

translucent   a translucent material allows some light through.

ventilation   fresh air circulating throughout a building.

zero-carbon   Zero carbon means no carbon dioxide is released into the atmosphere during a building's lifetime.

INDEX

LIST OF BUILDINGS AND ARCHITECTS FEATURED IN THIS BOOK

p.9 Burj Khalifa: Adrian Smith Skidmore, Owings & Merrill; p.9 Shanghai Tower: Gensler; p.9 Empire State Building: Shreve, Lamb and Harmon; p.9 One World Trade Center: David Childs Skidmore, Owings & Merrill; p.9 Patronas Twin Towers: César Pelli; p.9 Willis Tower: Bruce Graham and Fazlur Khan of Skidmore, Owings & Merrill; p.9 International Finance Centre: Pelli Clarke Pelli Architects; p.9 Shanghai World Financial Centre: Kohn Pedersen Fox; p.11 Habitat 67: Moshe Safdie; p.12 Casa Batlló: Antoni Gaudí; p.13 Chrysler Building: William Van Alen; p.14 Juscelino Kubitschek Bridge: Alexandre Chan; p.14 Golden Gate Bridge: Irving Morrow; p.14 Sydney Harbour Bridge: John Bradfiel; p.14 Millau Viaduct: architect Normal Foster and engineer Michel Virlogeux; p.15 Sendai Mediatheque: Toyo Ito; p.16 Heydar Aliyev Centre: Dame Zaha Hadid; p.17 Shanshui City design: Ma Yansong; p.20 Sydney Opera House: architect Jorn Utzon and engineer Ove Arup; p.21 National Museum of Qatar: Jean Nouvel; p.22 The Eden Project: Sir Nicholas Grimshaw; p.23 Paris Smart City 2050: Vincent Callebaut Architectures; p.24: 3D Printed House: Houben/Van Mierlo Architects, Van Wijnen; p.25 Riverside House: Shigeru Fuse Architects; p.26 Guggenheim Museum: Frank Lloyd Wright; p.27 Bilbao Guggenheim Museum: Frank Gehry; p.28 Yoga Pavilion: Elora Hardy, IBUKA; p.32 Villa E-1027: Eileen Gray; p.33 The Eames House: Charles and Ray Eames; p.37 Pyramids of Giza; p.37 The Great Ziggurt of Ur; p.37 Chichen Itza Pyramid; p.37 Nawarla Gabarnmung; p.38 Notre-Dame du Haut: Le Corbusier; p.39 Cliff Face House: Peter Stutchbury; p.42 Darling Square Library: Kengo Kumo; p.43 National Museum of African American History and Culture: Sir David Adjaye; p.44 Temple Mount; p.44 Amristar; p.44 Boudhanath; p.44 St Basil's Cathedral; p.45 Heddal Stave Church; p.46 Pantheon; p.47 Reichstag: Normal Foster, Foster + Partners; p.50 Beijing National Stadium: architects Jacques Herzog and Piere de Meuron, with artist consultant Ai Weiwei; p.51 The London Mastaba: Christo and Jeanne-Claude; p.54 Colosseum; p.54 Saint Peter's Basilica; p.54 Aqueduct of Segovia; p.55 Parthenon; p.56 Antares Tower: Odile Decq; p.56 Exhibition Information Centre: Odile Decq; p.57 The Walking City: Archigram & Ron Herron, and Oculus, Arts University Bournemouth: Sir Peter Cook; p.58 Women's Centre: Yasmeen Lari; p.61 Great Mosque of Djenne; p.62 Palais Bulles: Antti Lovag; p.63 The 'House of Bread': Coop Himmelb(l)au; p.64 Blur Building: Diller Scofidio + Renfro; p.65 SkyPark and Lotus Flower ArtScience Museum: Safdie Architects; p.66 Luum Temple: CO-LAB Design Office; p.67 Fungus Among Us: Eliana Nigro and Marc-Antoine Chartier-Primeau; p.69 Federation Square: LAB Architects & Bates Smart; p.70 Honeycomb Apartments: OFIS Architects; p.71 Royal Ontario Museum: Daniel Libeskind; p.72 CCTV Headquarters: Rem Koolhaas and Ole Scheeren, OMA Architects; p.73 Upside-down House: Klaudiusz Golos and Sebastian Mikiciu; p.73 Strawberry House; p.73 Kindergarten Wolfartsweier: Tomi Ungerer and Ayla Suzan Yöndel; p.74 Saint Peter's Basilica; p.75 Jean-Marie Tjibaou Cultural Centre: Renzo Piano; p.76 West Kowloon Station: Andrew Bromberg, Aedas; p.77 Arch of Septimius Severus; p.80 Inujima Art House Project: SANAA – Kazuyo Sejima & Ryue Nishizawa; p.81 Glass Pyramid at the Louvre: I M Pei; p.82 Centre Pompidou: Renzo Piano and Richard Rogers; p.83 Geisel Library: William Pereira; p.84 Princess Elisabeth Antarctica: Philippe Samyn and Partners; p.85 WaterNest: Giancarlo Zema; p.86 Angkor Wat; p.87 Old Bagan; p.88 Favela Painting Foundation: artists Hass&Hahn; p.89 Paper log house: Shigeru Ban; p.91 The Farmhouse model: Chris and Fei Precht; p.92 Sharp Centre for Design: Will Alsop and Young + Wright Architects; p.93 Nature Boardwalk, Lincoln Park Zoo: Jeanne Gang; p.94 Hawa Mahal; p.95 Neuschwanstein Castle; p.96 Morpheus Hotel: Zaha Hadid; p.97 Petersen Automotive Museum: Kohn Pedersen Fox; p.100 Taj Mahal: Ustad Ahmad Lahori; p.101 Buckminster Fuller Dome Home; p.102 Rietveld- Schröder House: Gerrit Rietveld; p.104 Sunflower House: Koichi Takada Architects; p.105 The High Line: James Corner Field Operations, Diller Scofidio + Renfro, and Piet Oudolf; p.106 Habitat: Kohn Pedersen Fox; p.106 Mars Simulation City: SEArch+/Apis Cor; p.108 Pod Playground: TCL landscape architects; p.108 Xylem: Diébédo Francis Kéré; p.108 Floating City: Vincent Callebaut; p.108 Hotel pod: Aidia Studio; p.108 Makoko Floating School: Kunlé Adeyemi.